Rufus W. Bailey

Addresses at the Inauguration of Rev. Rufus W. Bailey as President of Austin College

Anatiposi

Rufus W. Bailey

Addresses at the Inauguration of Rev. Rufus W. Bailey as President of Austin College

Reprint of the original.

1st Edition 2023 | ISBN: 978-3-38230-092-0

Anatiposi Verlag is an imprint of Outlook Verlagsgesellschaft mbH.

Verlag (Publisher): Outlook Verlag GmbH, Zeilweg 44, 60439 Frankfurt, Deutschland
Vertretungsberechtigt (Authorized to represent): E. Roepke, Zeilweg 44, 60439 Frankfurt, Deutschland
Druck (Print): Books on Demand GmbH, In de Tarpen 42, 22848 Norderstedt, Deutschland

ADDRESSES

AT

THE INAUGURATION

OF

REV. RUFUS W. BAILEY, A. M.

AS

PRESIDENT OF AUSTIN COLLEGE,

HUNTSVILLE, TEXAS.

FEBRUARY 10, 1859.

HOUSTON:
PRINTED AT THE TELEGRAPH BOOK AND JOB ESTABLISHMENT.
1859.

The services were introduced by the reading of a portion of Scripture, and prayer by the President. A. M. BRANCH, Esq., as Chairman of the Executive Committee, and on the part of the Trustees, addressed a large audience assembled in the College Chapel, and delivered the Keys, the Ensigns of Office, to the President.

ADDRESS
OF A. M. BRANCH, ESQ.

LADIES AND GENTLEMEN—

The occasion which calls us together, is full of interest·
Where Nature displays her beauties, there Science should build
her temple, and upon this consecrated spot, hallowed by so
many pleasing associations of the past, we have come up to renew
our efforts in the great cause of Learning. Taking fresh courage
from the circumstances by which we are surrounded, we are in·
spired with confidence in the final triumph of our enterprise, and
we behold the cloud which has lowered over us for a while, rolling
away beyond us, and the rainbow of returning hope bending over
us in the bright promise of the future.

We have met to-night to inaugurate the President of Austin
College,—to invest him with the insignia of his high office, and,
to bid him God speed in conducting this, our cherished Institution,
towards that renown which awaits it, in the future.

Our people, too, well know that without public virtue and intelligence there can be no security for the permanency of our re-
publican institutions, and consequently no effort has been spared
to advance the great cause of popular enlightenment.

Knowledge is now carried to the humble dwelling of the poor
as well as the splendid mansion of the rich ; like the sun in his
glory, it diffuses its light indiscriminately, and consequently all are
enlightened. Indeed the present is an age of Science and Litera-
ture. In every department of Learning and the Arts, our country

commands the respect and admiration of the world.

Although we may yet be deficient in those things which form the peculiar charm of the Ancients, and which are said to constitute the elements of classical interest and beauty, yet in every thing susceptible of improvement we have left them far behind ; we can truly boast of the Eloquence of our Orators, the Wisdom of our Statesmen, of the various Literary and Scientific Institutions that adorn and beautify our land as thickly and as beautifully as the stars of the firmament. Nature herself has not only founded our country on the grandest scale, but it is inhabited by a people who exhibit, in all their modes of thought and principles of action, a beautiful moral resemblance to the boldness of the natural scenery by which they are surrounded. It is written in the history of other countries that they have fallen, through the corruption of ambitious rulers, who imposed upon the credulity of the people ; but ours presents the splendid example of a nation which, though yet in its infancy, has assumed a position the proudest and the first among the powers of the earth.

This lofty eminence has not been attained by the rapid develment of its physical resources alone, but by the energy of mind awakened by a liberal system of Education among the masses. The Science of Government can only be understood, and civil and religious liberty preserved, by those lessons of wisdom taught in the Schools. It is here that the history, the progress, the rise and fall of other nations are made known ; and here, too, is taught how evanescent are the trifles by which popular favor is often acquired, and how easily lost; and that true distinction can only be attained by a rare combination of intellect, eloquence and virtue.

Though it is not my intention on this occasion to make a speech, I can not refrain from expressing the gratification which I feel in beholding so many young men, whose position in life, whose opportunities for improvement, have marked them out as belonging to that class into whose hands, in after-times, the destiny of our beloved Country is to be committed. It is to your care, Sir. these youthful minds must be indebted for that mental training which will enable them to act well their parts in the great drama of life. The Board of Trustees of Austin College, having full confidence in your judgment and great learning, have, by a unanimous vote. placed you at the head of this Institution. The promptness with which the public, as with one voice, have approved of their action, is an indication of the success with which your efforts will be crowned. As a member of the Executive Committee, whose humble representative I am, I now surrender into your hands the keys of this Institution,—and, as they unlock the entrance into this edifice. so may you, and those with whom you are associated, by lessons of wisdom, impart to the Students of this Institution, the key by which they may gain access to the vast storehouse of knowledge in the records of the present and the past, and, in their turn, enrich the world with imperishable trophies of minds here trained and developed under your culture.

REPLY

AND ADDRESS OF THE PRESIDENT.

Sir,—I receive these keys, extended by you in a manner too flattering, as indicating and conferring, *in form*, the authority under which I have already acted *in fact*. In assuming the responsibilities of this office, I enter on the discharge of duties, with which, I may say, my course of life has rendered me long familiar. I bring also, and consecrate to the services of Austin College whatever of talent, acquirement, capacity or energy I may possess, all is earnestly devoted.

LADIES AND GENTLEMEN, FELLOW CITIZENS ALL.—Your attention is now solicited to some facts and considerations which I desire distinctly to announce at this time and in this place.

Austin College, which occupies our affections and concentrates our labors, embraces already, in its history, passages of absorbing interest. Like him whose name it bears, it takes its place as a pioneer in this new Empire State. Its charter dates on the 22nd day of November, 1849, and the first class was graduated in June, 1854. This, then, was the first College chartered, and the class of '54 the first College class graduated in Texas.

The present appears to me a fit occasion to place on record the story of its birth, its baptism, its early struggles, trials and triumphs—so that when, in the rapid flight of time, these native forests, now melting away, with the log cabins of the first generations, are supplanted by cereal grains and rich cotton fields and palaces, the homes of refinement, luxury and intelligence—when the youth of other generations, seeking instruction here shall walk these academic groves and sit under the shade of trees which we are seeking to plant and cultivate for posterity ; the shade trees indicative of civilization, scions taken it may be from the forest, but improved by education under our culture—when the shadowy past is gathering on the history of Austin College, now the child of our labors and our love, but then a century old and honored by its sons in every department of life and labor in this Empire State—when, I say, these changes shall have come over the primitive forests and fields which we have painfully wrought and cultivated, and that noble army of our sons, now unborn, rising up in long perspective to inherit from us, shall lean against the structures of our workmanship and ask, "who planted these trees ? Who laid these foundations ? Who built this seat of learning ?"—then, yes, then, the men of this generation will come into remembrance, and some of those who may descend from us may be proud to trace their genealogy, and glory in the names they may bear, of Baker, or Chase, or Yoakum, or Smith, or Sorley, or others of their ancestry who, in the history preserved in these archives, shall be recognized among the men who devised liberal things and came up with their counsels, their money and their prayers to found and organize. and preserve and perpetuate Austin College when it was in the weakness of infancy and un-noted in the general rush for good lands and personal gains. Now, when in our extremity, having labored almost to exhaustion, we call upon Hercules, the men to be remembered, are those who come in such a time as this. Let other men receive the honor that may be due them in all times—men who may endow the tenth or the twentieth professorship, who may add cumulative life and vigor to Austin College as it will be hereafter. We propose to post up to the present time, to write out and deposit in the iron safe of this young Hercules, the history of the past, and seek to place at the head of honored benefactors, those to whose labors and wisdom this Institution owes, under God, its existence. Let others take the honor of administering to its manhood—these have brought it to the birth and nursed its infancy.

First, then, we may say, the man who made a place for us here by his enterprise, labors and sufferings, gives name to AUSTIN COLLEGE. Then, its real founder, without whose untiring efforts and prayers, and indomitable perseverence it never would have had a local "habitation and a name," is recognized in the BAKER PROFESSORSHIP. Then the noble man, who listened to the successful agent and really made, under the circumstances, a princely donation to ensure success, gives name to the CHASE PROFESSORSHIP.*

There is another name, which deserves a place where it may be emblazoned through all time, on this bright page of our history, Col. HENDERSON YOAKUM was a man of forecast, of prudence and energy, a counselor of a large heart and liberal mind. To him and to the devotion of his well directed labors, Austin College owes a debt hardly second in extent to any other due to any other man. His vitality was instinct with a power to impress-animate and control others, and while he comprehended widely by intuition, he had the power to influence men by a wisdom as modestly expressed as it was luminous and logical. Had he lived the life of the College would never have been suspended.

There is a record, too, which shall be preserved embracing the names of others who have freely and liberally contributed to erect this monument to the enterprise of the early Texas emigrants, who have evinced that they deemed a provision for the education of their children and their neighbors' children an object worthy of sacrifices. Those who shall descend from them shall know them, What their ancestors have worthily done shall be a part of their inheritance, and the good deeds here performed shall live with moral power to energize character in the line of their posterity to the thousandth generation.

* See Appendix A.

We often hear of "blood" and of "stock" as applied to the race of man as well as of horses or of cattle. I believe in it. But I think it flows principally in a moral channel of transmission. The deeds and character of ancestors live in the traditions of families, are there treasured and imitated. If noble, they energize the minds that are linked to them by inheritance. If ignoble, they are naturally excused or received as examples "leaning to virtue's side." Hence "like begets like." Every family has its history. If not emblazoned by heraldry or the written page, yet transmitted by tradition, sought after, treasured in the memory, pregnant with life and power to influence others in a long line of those who may come after them. Character is inherited as truly as property or poverty.

Every man connects himself with his ancestry. We all feel this and own it. When, four years ago, I emigrated to Texas, I paid my last visit to my father-land, and read with intense interest the history of my ancestors traced back to Plymouth Rock through eight generations. I took my final leave of my mother, then in her eighty-eighth year—who did more to make me what I have been, what I am, and whatever I may be, than all other earthly influences together. Her instructions distilled like dew upon my early pathway, then fragrant with flowers and bright in the sunrise of life. These lessons have stood before me permanent forms at every step for more than half a century. They are the paving stones, "saxa viva" "lively stones," like the foundations of the city of the New Jerusalem. They have reflected light from heaven, guided my life and shaped its ends. Her image has been ever before me, smiling when others frowned as she smiled on my childhood. My children know her in her lessons repeated to them as they were committed to me, and these lessons will have their influence transmitted through generations that may never know her. Such, in part, is the formation and transmission of character. "History is philosophy teaching by example."

2

We will seek to place before the minds we may here contribute to mould and expand, the character of the men by whose
labors, self-denials and sacrifices, they have been introduced to
these classic walks and privileged sources of education—men who
believed and acted on the belief, that they were made for a world
which was made for them—unselfish men, who felt that their em-
inent ability to do good was intended by a munificent Providence
to insure to the benefit of other men as well as themselves, whose
question of duty was, not so much " What good will all this do
me?" as that other question of divine origin—"what good will
all this do to my race, and how may it redound to the glory of
God ?"

We will ever keep before the minds of the youth who may
resort here for instruction, that the founders and early friends of
Austin College were religious men—men of prayer, whose liberal charities came warm gushing from souls who waited daily in
devotion at that throne whence issue the streams of divine love,
and the light that shines with exceeding brightness on the evil
and on the good.

The early history of Austin College shows that it was the
child of prayer, and traces its paternity to praying men.* As
early as the year 1840, the Rev. Daniel Baker, while acting as
a missionary in Texas, directed public attention to the endowment and location of a College. His return to the States inter-
rupted the prosecution of his plans, and it was not until 1848,
that the Brazos Presbytery took the subject earnestly in hand and
appointed Dr. Baker their agent to take up subscriptions and
prosecute the enterprise. In less than three years this agency
resulted in the collection of $20,000 in money, and 15,000 acres
of land. Huntsville was selected as the site of the College, and
this elegant and commodious building which we now occupy

* See Appendix B.

was erected and paid for by public subscription at a cost of $16,000. The Rev. Samuel McKinney was the first President, and took possession of the College edifice in 1852. He resigned the Presidency in the following year and the Rev. Dr. Baker was elected in his place. Dr. Baker entered on his duties as Presiding officer, in December of the same year, but still continued with unremitting labors and eminent success, his efforts as general agent until 1856, when he resigned the Presidency, but still continued his agency. In the Autumn of 1857, he attended on the meeting of the Legislature at Austin, to prosecute a memorial before that body for an appropriation in aid of the College. His great labor and earnest anxiety at last proved to be too much, even for his constitution, naturally robust, yet now less able than formerly to sustain the sleepless and ceaseless labors of an ardent and impassioned soul in keen pursuit of a great object. He sunk suddenly under heart-throbs too violent for the strength of a clay tenement, as well constructed for its purposes as any, perhaps, that ever labored for 68 years, but not strong enough then to sustain the action of his great soul, expanded and struggling under the pressure of his grand subject. He died on the 10th day of December, 1857, and was buried with public honors. The Legislature adjourned to attend his funeral, and passed resolutions of regret and sympathy. His remains are to be removed and placed under a suitable monument to commemorate his name in this enclosure. This column shall be the first object that meets the eye in the access to Austin College, while it may be present in the daily walks of the successive generations of students in all time to come. His Memoirs, faithfully collated and published by his son, may perpetuate his character and inculcate his spirit in the recitation room and closet of every professor and every student. Thus are we excited to great and good deeds by great and good men, whom we learn to love and revere. That book will never go out of print. That monument, I shall consider it a part of my duty as his immediate successor in office, to keep before the public attention till it is completed, and the marble column shall rise, suitably engraved to fill our grand idea of perpetuating the virtues of the man, when we, who knew him well, shall be no longer here to tell them to our children's children.

After the death of Dr. Baker, the Presidency remained vacant until the 15th of December last, when his successor was appointed. In the mean time, under a combination of difficulties, the exercises of the College were suspended, and resumed under a new organization on the 6th day of February, 1859.

This forms the first chapter in the history of Austin College. Under a liberal Charter from the Legislature of the State, granted on the petition of the Brazos Presbytery, it stands in immediate relation to the Synod of Texas, by whom all vacancies that may occur in the Board of Trustees are filled.

I but state a historical fact when I say that Presbyterians plant the Church and the Schoolhouse wherever they emigrate, wherever they abide. Wherever, in a new country, " they lift up the axe mightily upon trees." there the log cabin, the meeting-house, and the school house spring forth from the forest, and are raised in succession by the first labors of their hands. They do not wait to become rich before they contribute to these objects—they contribute to these objects that they may be rich. Everywhere, and always, they have been the liberal patrons of learning, the unflinching advocates of an open Bible, of religious liberty, a separation of Church and State, and universal toleration. Hence, in the organization of this College, as of all their Schools and Colleges, intended to unite a general patronage, the only claim they have asserted, is for an open Bible and an exposition of the great principles of morals as there defined.

When we speak of Austin College as founded in prayer by religious men, and for religious educatian, we do not mean that it is, or was, designed to be any thing else than a Literary Institution for the cultivation of the intellect—but certainly the cultivation of the mind in all its powers, faculties and relations, laws, responsibilities and obligations. The cultivation, then, of the moral sense, of the religious element of our nature, which holds us to the Throne of God must be essential to a well-balanced mind and necessary to secure its efforts in the right direction.

It is impossible to educate an intelligent being without a recognition and training of the moral sense. Every action of life, and of death, involve moral relations, emotions and duties, and we can not separate the mental activities from the moral emotions. Religion is a necessity for beings religiously constituted—and we are such, and can not deny ourselves. We may try to do it, but our convictions lie deeper than our infidelity. We can not persuade ourselves that we are blind by shutting our eyes. Any theory of education, that overlooks or leaves out of account the moral man, must lay its foundation in the sand. The storms of passion will uproot and desolate that superstructure. It is idle to talk of separating literary education from the religious sentiment, the cultivation of the intellect from the conscience. The child that is divided to satisfy the claims of two contending mothers, is murdered —and so is the boy whose intellect is educated at the expense of his heart. The steam engine is a power, but destructive, "destroying others, by itself destroyed," when not directed and controlled —so is the human intellect when inflamed and heated by the passions, but escaped from moral restraint.

A College is, of necessity, under the control of religious men or irreligious men. Our sons will be taught—they must be taught, by men that are religious or irreligious. Do you send out your sons unwarned, and therefore unarmed, into the world with all their senses awake to all the objects embraced in their field of vision, with their passions vigorous and virulent, with their mental activities in restless action, inexperienced, unsuspecting and depraved by nature—do you dismiss them from their home and expect to return unchanged, unstained, made better as they acquire knowledge by travel and study and contact with the world? Fatal error! A father of seven sons once said to me—"When my two eldest boys were educated. I sought to separate them from all religious influences that might affect their opinions. I selected a College for them least likely, as I thought, to interfere with my liberal purposes, where the Professors were men of "no religion." After their graduation and return home, I presented them each with a Bible, and requested their particular study of it to form their independent religious opinions. What was my astonishment to find that the enemy had anticipated me and sown tares. They were infidels already." Since, then, I say, it is impossible for men to live and think without religious convictions, to direct, strengthen and train minds naturally constituted religious is the part of education. Neglect to cultivate your gardens, and weeds will exhaust the soil. So certainly will souls that are without the cultivation of the religious principle, be *atheoi*, atheists.

We hold that the education of a human being should be adapted to his entire constitution and suited to the whole duration of his being. The cultivation of his intellect, ruled and controlled by his passions, would make him worse than before. The affections, left without the influence of a well instructed judgment, would mistake their proper objects. The mind and heart, then, must be suitably disciplined, and taught to act in harmony and correspondence.

Here we take our stand. We demand for our sons an education on religious principles—an education which seeks first and always to correct the moral disorders of the heart, and then to give knowledge, vigor and activity to the mental energies, restrained by the centripetal force of an enlightened and tender conscience. Youth can not be adequately controlled by any other discipline. An enlightened and educated conscience secures a ready subjection to good laws. Intellect, cultivated at the expense of the moral sense, gives power to do evil with no corresponding restraint. Hence the schools which have been best sustained in this country have ever been those organized under religious supervision and controlled by religious men. Such must always be the case. The experiment has been repeatedly made and the problem solved. Texas has followed in the wake of older States but after their example in the construction of denominational schools—Austin College by the Presbyterians, Baylor University by the Baptists, and Soule University by the Methodists. Yet neither of these intitutions teach theology, much less sectarian doctrines. They are all, however, religious institutions in the sense of making religion the basis of their theory of education, and in that sense only.

For Austin College, founded by the labors of Presbyterians—organized, watched and watered under the supervision of the Synod of Texas, a monument of their zeal and pious effort in the cause of learning, we claim that its entire construction has been made with reference to a wholesome religious influence in the education of our youth. We do not teach Presbyterianism, but we do seek to lead the minds of our young men to "fear God and keep his commandments"—to feel their obligations to God as the only security to fidelity in their duties to men. We desire it to be distinctly understood that the young men, who are educated here, have been made to feel a religious influence by "line upon line and precept upon precept." When we cannot occupy this ground, we shall retire from the labors of education, believing that all we can do without it would be worse than nothing.

The religious aspects of this College, then, and the objects at which we aim, are patent and palpable. While we enforce no dogmas and seek to instill no creed, we do seek to educate our youth religiously. The Bible is installed as a text-book—that is our creed—God's written constitution for the government of our race, the great moral code of the universe, the revealed will of the King of Kings. We educate our sons to read it, to value it, to have it. It lies on our desk where we all assemble in this College morning and evening—the only classic thus installed as pertaining to all in common. We read it in two lessons a day, all assembled together, and seek for divine light and divine teaching that this Word of Life may be understood. We then send our pupils away with the admonition that they are individually responsible to God for their own interpretation of His law and for the regulation of all their action under it—that they must give an account to God for all the deeds done in the body, each for himself and not another. We have in our Library, one Bible for every student in the Institution, subject to his use. We have a Bible Class on the Sabbath, at which every member of the College is required to be present and discuss in the most unconstrained manner a portion of God's Word previously assigned. Thus we seek to exert a religious, not a sectarian influence. The man, who does not wish to have his son so trained and taught, will seek out some other agency to aid in his course of education. But in this we believe we meet the mind of the people, for we are a religious people.

In providing for the instruction required in our course of study, we seek to employ religious men—men of high moral tone, who may impress themselves on the young mind and give a safe direction to it—men of might to stand at these fountains of influence and give direction to the streams that issue thence. That done, no religious test of sectarian mould is applied. No religious faith is required of students, and no effort permitted to proselyte them to any religious creed. They are required to attend in an orderly manner on the religious services of the Sabbath, but at the church of their own choice, and to worship God according to the dictates of their own consciences.

In our theory, then, the basis of all sound education lies in the parallel and coincident training of the mind and the heart, of the intellect and moral sense, not neglecting a physical discipline that will present the "mens sana in corpore sano." In Texas, however, where our youth live so much out of doors, and are early attracted by the hunt and the chase with horse and hound—where they are conversant with the wide-extended paternal acres, and where an ordinary neighborhood of families embraces a territory equal in area to a common principality of the old world, a healthy constitution of physical habits naturally fostered, renders attention to physical discipline less a matter of definite education. Yet even here we encourage athletic exercises in the campus and gymnasium, suited to the leisure hour and intervals of study. Our principal labor, however, lies in leading to mental application, acquisition and discipline.

This, then, is our introduction to a new era in the history of Austin College. With the lights of past experience, an improved and improving condition of our finances, a Faculty devoted exclusively to the duties of the recitation and lecture-room, we need only the material, rough-hewn, on which to try our hand and prove our skill.

Let parents give us their children, the brothers in Austin College, and the sisters in Andrew Female College, another well-organized Institution,—which gracefully adorns the opposite hill,—not under our control, but holding our confidence and having our sympathies—and we may confidently hope that the happy parents may, in due time, receive back again "their sons as plants grown up in their youth, their daughters as corner-stones polished after the similitude of a palace."

3

ADDRESS*

OF

HON. P. W. KITTRELL,

MEMBER OF THE BOARD.

————•————

My Audience :—There is an instinctive, an influential and abiding principal in the breast of man which prompts him to seek for knowledge, to desire to be educated   We see it evinced in every stage of our being.   This prompts us continually to seek and desire the unattained and unknown.   I was struck with the remark of one of the speakers who preceded (Mr. Branch,) " that it was the province of science to know no limits." My mind instantly associated with that idea, the one, that the capacity of the human mind knows no limits. A distinguished philosopher, I believe it was La Place, said : " that which we know is little—that which we know not is immense." The principle above alluded to, stimulates our curiosity and calls out our powers of research and investigation to the fullest extent of their capacity. All that we have acquired, that is new, or useful, or profitable, in our former researches or investigations, only seems to increase the desire to explore the unknown. The good of the present only seems to lead the mind to desire the larger and more indefinite treasures of the future, and the human mind by this process, is continually expansive and expanding, goes on to live in brighter scenes, and enrich itself with new treasures.

————* This address, like Col. Branche's, is an abstract, or condensed form of what was delivered.

Long before the discovery of America, the early *maritime adventurers*, standing on the Canaries and the Azores, fancied they descried land in the far west. They, in fact, made no such discovery. But it was no extraordinary refraction of the rays of light, no ocean mirage which deceived them. The images, it is true, were illusive. But it was that intense desire, that longing after the unattained and unknown which deceived them. This same principle lies at the foundation of all our undertakings, and properly directed and educated, the life and soul of all our enterprises—religious, benevolent and educational.

It was the practical working of this principal which led to the building of this beautiful college edifice. Its founders had their eyes fixed on the future of their children—their country—the churches. And in so looking, they engaged in the work of rearing a college that, begining as it were, with the very infancy of our young, growing and interesting State, should expand into full and symmetrical proportions as our society should advance to maturity. They contemplated the work not only in its probable and, I may say, almost certain beneficial results and influences in society, when it should be completed; but in the difficulties and trials which they would have to encounter in its incipiency and completion. They knew, as the worthy President has told you to-night, it was not the work of a moment, or a day, or a year, to found such an institution : they knew that years of anxious toil and unrewarded solicitude would be required to complete their labors.

Here it may not be inappropriate to enquire, who who was foremost in the work of erecting on the summit of this hill, this Pioneer temple of science? who first crossed the almost fabled Sabine, and penetrated this wild country, scarcely then rescued from the wild beast and savage, and conceived this noble design? Who, endowed seemingly with a spirit of intuition, anticipated the wants of this vast Empire State of ours? Whose soul-stirring philanthrophy, and indomitable energy prompted him to this deed? I need not tell you that it was Dan'l Baker, a name I never now mention except with a kind of melancholy reverence. No! I see these questions already answered by the saddened countenances of this audience. Though his remains now lie shrouded in the gloomy habiliaments of the grave in a neighboring city, yet he is deeply enshrined in our hearts and our memories, and long after that monumental shaft which you have been told to-night, will be erected on this hill to his memory, shall have mouldered into dust, will he be reme mbered as the faithful minister, the warm-hearted philanthrophist, the friend and benefactor of learning, in short, the man who ever dared to live for purposes worthy of a man and a christian ; and I trust that Austin College may long stand as a proud and useful monument of his industry, his energy and his philanthrophy.

To his successor in office, it now becomes my duty as one of the Trustees of the college, and on their behalf, to address myself.

To you, sir, is committed the charge of this Institution of learning ; you have been appointed to this position by the confidence and suffrage of the *whole board of trustees* ; your position is honorable and useful, not only from the intimate relations which you sustain to the Board of Trustees, to the Faculty, your associates in teaching to the students and patrons of the institution, but also, from the character of the work which you are called on to perform. "Men of genius and enterprise have devoted their lives to the mingling of colors, and blending lights and shades on canvass, or in moulding the lifeless marble into the shape of. man, or investing it with interest in some other way. Their deeds have been made the subject of historic record, and the burden of the poets' song. But the resistless and unsparing tooth of time has doomed them both to destruction, because the material on which they impressed their skill as well as that which contained their record was perishable."

But, sir, yours will necessarily be more lasting ; you will have to impress your skill on the inextinguishable intellect, the immortal minds of men, which are imperishable. The corroding tooth of time can never efface your work. No, sir, if properly done and sanctified and directed by the grace of God, hundreds of youths who may go forth from this college, as they climb the steep, where " fame's proud temple shines afar, and after they shall have attained the proud summit, will point to you, sir, and this their *alma mater*, and say : by your help '*exegi monumentum*, perennium *aere.*" ' A Grecian artist was once asked, why he devoted so much time to a single work of his pencil ? his reply was : " I paint for eternity." In a much higher and more appropriate sense, may you and your associates in the great business of teaching, say : " We paint for eternity."

You have immortal minds committed to your care. Every impression here made on the mind, every mental effort or activity called forth, all moral or mental expansion in whatever form, will be as lasting as the imperishable minds which you teach. The character of your work gives honor to your position, from the fact, as you have justly said to-night, that you intend to " prosecute it within the claims, and according to the true morality of the Bible ;" a sentiment, sir, worthy of your calling. And here I may be permitted to add my humble endorsement to that sentiment and determination of yours ; for I have been long, since convinced, that it is only when agencies, *human* and *divine*, operate in unison, cultivating the intellect and the moral elements of our nature and the better feelings and affections of our heart, that education can be made a blessing to mankind.

Another thought which the occasion suggests, is, that your position, though honorable, is one of heavy responsibility and attended with great difficulties. You have a great variety of minds to operate upon. Associations of this kind must necessarily bring together a variety of elements, each member of which has some peculiarity of mind, manners and disposition, to which attention must be paid in the administration of the government of your institution. For no association of this kind can succeed—can operate harmoniously and successfully without a proper system of discipline; a large share of practical, sound wisdom, founded upon a knowledge of human character is necessary in adapting proper rules and regulations to the peculiarities of each and all of who may be placed under your care. Promptness and decision, combined with prudent forbearance are also necessary to secure the ends of government. Your position is important and difficult, from the peculiar nature of the business of teaching. In consequence of the great variety of minds you have to operate on, your instruction, or rather mode of instruction, must be so varied, as to suit the temper, disposition and peculiarities of each. The timid and self-distrusting must be encouraged, and inspired with a laudable ambition for success. The forward and self-reliant must be taught to know that self-confidence will not supersede a long course of laborious industry and persevering toil. The indolent and inactive must be stimulated to study and close application. The excitable and impatient, to close investigation and patient thought. This whole work is to be so performed as to be suited to the peculiarities of all, so as to render the business of teaching and governing successful in the developement of the whole man, moral, mental and physical, in all the symmetrical strength and beauty of which he is susceptible, so as to fit him for the highest circles of distinction and usefulness in human society.

The last thought which I shall present, is, that however arduous your work, it has its rewards; and this reflection should be a stimulus to every noble and virtuous purpose connected with the proper discharge of duty, as well as the sweetener of all your cares and toils. You have your reward in the confidence and co-operation of the board of *trustees,* and your associates in the work of instruction ; in the confidence and sympathy of the imperishable minds under your care, and that of the patrons and the friends of the institution and learning generally. And I sincerely hope, sir, that you may have your reward in the final success, which may crown your labors. I trust, sir, that thousands of youth may go forth from these academic walks, deeply and thoroughly imbued with the love of science and knowledge, well qualified to fight successfully, usefully and honorably, the great battle of life—and that it may ever be one of the pleasures of their life, to cherish a grateful reminisence of you, and this, their *Alma Mater*.

Then, sir, you will have your reward in the consciousness of having consecrated those noble gifts of Providence with which you have been blessed, together with your distinguished acquirements, the fruits of many years of application and toil, to the good of society, in laboring to diffuse the light of knowlege through community, and prepare youth for the highest degree of usefulness here, and the highest standard of happiness hereafter.

APPENDIX.

A.

The design and liberal purposes of Mr. Chase may be seen in the following extract from a letter now on file in the College archives, directed to Col. H. Yoakum, one of the Trustees, dated Natches, April 24, 1851.

"I purchased the lands with the intention of removing to Texas, and devoting my life to the welfare of the people, and obtained a certificate of citizenship. New difficulties soon arose throughout the country, my voice failed, and I was laid aside from preaching. There was no longer any inducement to leave a home of comfort and competence, and I abandoned all idea of removing there. But I never abandoned the desire to do what I could to promote the temporal and eternal welfare of the people of Texas. In 1833, I supplied Austin's Colony and the district of Nacogdoches with the Bible, devoted several months to the work, and was probably the first Protestant Minister that ever preached a sermon in Texas. From exposure in swimming streams, lying wet, &c., I lost the use of my right arm for several months. I merely allude to these things to show that I have been the uniform friend of Texas. In devoting all my valuable interests there towards the endowment of an institution of learning, I wished to do it in such a manner as would best promote the end.

4

" Remembering that the Trustees may be pressed for funds in recting the buildings, and wishing to have the avails of the lands chiefly applied to the erection of necessary buildings, and the remainder toward the endowment of Professorships, I have concluded to execute a deed allowing twenty per cent. of the avails to be applied to the erection of necessary buildings, and the remainder toward the endowment of Professorships."

In reply to a letter written to him by Dr. Baker, President of the College, Mr. Chase says, of date Feb. 6, 1856.

" The restraint imposed is not against the sale of any or all the lands, but against appropriating more than twenty per cent. of the sales to the erection of buildings, purchase of books, apparatus, &c., so as to interfere with the endowment of a professorship. My object in bestowing the land was the permanent benefit of the Institution—and in my judgment, that object will be better promoted by securing a Professorship than by the further erection of buildings at present, if the avails of the lands are inadequate to the accomplishment of both ; and, therefore, that the restriction had better remain unaltered. Experience will probably show that it is easier to provide for the accommodation of students than to secure able and permanent Professors, without a competent and certain support."

A part of the lands given by Mr. Chase, have been recently sold, and the money invested, more than sufficient to endow the CHASE PROFESSORSHIP. Thus is the benevolent purpose of this first and principal donor to the funds of Austin College fully met, leaving a large quantity of land included in his deed of gift, to accrue in the benefit of the College,

APPENDIX.

B.

The origin and endowment of Austin College may be seen by consulting the "Life and Labors of Daniel Baker," by which it will be seen also, that most of the contributions came warm from the hearts of new converts brought into the church under his preaching, placed in his hand as an agent for the College, an offering with prayer for this infant Institution, before its foundations were laid. It was sustained, too, to the day of his death by similar contributions to his faithful labors in the ministry, for which he made, for six successive years, missions to the churches in "the States," having sought in vain for aid from the Legislature of Texas.

He says, page 395, "At the Fall meeting of the Presbytery, (1848) held, I think, in Washington, the subject of establishing a Presbyterian College in Texas, was brought up. Something had been done, but not efficiently. Rev. Mr. M'Cullough had, about two years before, been sent on to the North as agent, and had obtained a considerable number of books, and money to the amount of about $500. But Goliad having been the place fixed upon, and this location not having been much approved of, the matter was permitted to remain without any further action."

On page 402, he says, "I had as yet never been in Huntsville, Walker county, middle Texas, but having heard a favorable account of the place, I went there and held a protracted meeting, which lasted a few days. As this meeting drew to a close, I mentioned to some of the prominent citizens that the Presbytery of Brazos had resolved to take measures for the establishment of a Presbyterian College somewhere in middle Texas. I told them I was pleased with Huntsville, and wished to know if the citizens desired the College to be established there. Subscription papers were put in circulation, and in a few days, some $8,000 were subscribed 'for the erection and support of a College by the Presbyterian church at, or within a mile of Huntsville, Walker county, Texas, to be called Baker College.'"

On page 406-7, he says, "At my request, Col. H. Yoakum drew up the charter of the College, making such alterations as I suggested. At the next meeting of the Presbytery, which was held at Independence, the charter was submitted—and a committee was appointed to secure the needful charter. When the naming of the institution was called up, I found that there was a communication from the original subscribers requesting the Presbytery to sanction the name originally given. I again declined the honor proposed to be done me. The matter was discussed, and the Institution was named AUSTIN COLLEGE, in honor of Stephen F. Austin, the great Texas pioneer."

On page 430, he says, "On the 6th day of April, 1850, I was appointed permanent agent. Shortly after, I received, first a verbal, and then a written communication from Rev. BENJAMIN CHASE, of Natches, Mississippi, stating that he had some lands in Texas, which he was willing to donate to the College. This was the rising of the morning star upon our noble enterprise. Soon after, he writes from New Orleans, page 433, "I have succeeded in my agency far beyond my most sanguine expectations. Besides remitting $377, there are good subscriptions for $500 or

$600 more." Writing from Savannah soon after, he says—" I have set my heart upon making Huntsville. as far as I have influence, the Athens of Texas, in building up there a College of high character, one that shall be a credit to Texas and an honor to the Presbyterian name."

On page 441, he says—" On this tour, I obtained books. maps, globes and subscriptions in money to the amount of $4,165. I went to Natches, saw brother CHASE, and received from him a relinquishment of all the lands which he owned in Texas, amounting to nearly 15,000 acres. Upon my return to Texas, I succeeded in securing lands to the College valued at $25,000."

In 1851, he goes North on his *second* tour, and writes on his return (p. 445,) " My tour has been upon the whole, quite successful—something more than $2,000 in money. Besides this, the "Texas Emigrating Company" of Louisville, Kentucky, have donated to Austin College, $1,000, in a certain contingency, with the probability of that amount being trebled." " A donation was also made in New York of a fine philosophical apparatus, which cost $800, by a distinguished philanthropist, an elder in Dr. Phillips' church, Wall street."

The result of his *third* tour, principally in South Carolina, through a series of revivals, is recorded on page 479,—" Free will offerings to the College poured in in a wonderful manner· Heavy remittances were sent home. It was one check after another! The whole amounting, I think, to nearly $6,000.

His *fourth* tour, through a similar course of revivals, is thus summed up on page 500,—" I have sent home more than $4,400, and have on hand more than $1,500." Records like the following fill his letters :—" Hearts opened—purses have been opened, also, and in some cases, the silvery stream flowing in has been swollen to such an extent that I had to check it! How thankful should I be that the Lord has so abundantly blessed my labors of love; for if I had not been blessed in my preaching, I should never have been so successful in my agency.

His *fifth* and *sixth* tours were confined to Texas—"It is time," he said, " that Texas should pass her minority and act for herself, I am ashamed longer to beg abroad. Here his efforts were confined to the endowment of the Baker Professorship of Mathematics, and the Chase Professorship of Languages. On July 1, '57, he writes thus :—" Our endowment scheme goes on swimmingly. During my trip of some five weeks in eastern Texas, I obtained subscriptions to the amount of $1,600. During my more recent trip to Galveston, Columbia, &c., I obtained for the College in notes and land to the amount of some $4,300. The whole amount added to the resources of the College since January last, is something like $26,000. This includes sales of land given by Rev. Benj. Chase, to amount of $15,000, and invested in coupon bonds."

The good man then turned his attention again to the Legislature of Texas, assembled in the Fall at Austin, and there died knocking at the door of the Capitol.

Such is the origin, such the history of Austin College. Is it not the child of prayer, founded by religious men, by the free will offerings of the church in her harvest-home, of her children in their bridal ?

TRUSTEES.

Rev. RUFUS W. BAILEY, Ex-officio President.
" J. W. MILLER,
" R. H. BYERS,
Hon. SAM HOUSTON,
Col. JOHN HILL,
WM. A. STEWART, Esq.,
J. CARROL SMITH, Esq.,
A. M. BRANCH, Esq.,
JAMES SORLEY, Esq.,
Col. JOHN HUME,
D. McGREGOR, Esq.,
A. J. BURKE, Esq.,
Rev. JAMES WILSON,
" P. H. FULLENWIDER,
Dr. J. A. LAWRENCE,
Hon. P. W. KITTRELL.

J. M. FULLENWIDER, Librarian.
S. C. ROUNTREE, Esq., Treasurer.

THE PRESIDENCY.

Rev. SAMUEL McKINNEY,
Elected President, April 5, 1850 ; resigned June 29, 1853.

Rev. DANIEL BAKER, D. D.,
Elected President, June 29, 1853 ; resigned Jan'y 16, 1857.
Prof. A. E. THOM,
Acting President, from Jan'y 16, 1857, to June 24, 1858.
Rev. RUFUS W. BAILEY,
Elected President, December 15, 1858.

FACULTY.

Rev. RUFUS W. BAILEY, A. M., President,
Professor of Moral and Intellectual Philosophy.
Rev. JOSEPH H. CALVIN, A. M.,
Professor of Ancient and Modern Languages.
JOSEPH H. PENTECOST, A. B.,
Prof. provisional, of Mathematics and Natural Science.
WM. F. PERRIE, A. B.,
Prof. adjunct of Latin and Greek Languages.

Profs. PERRIE & PENTECOST,
In charge of Preparatory Department, *pro tempore.*

ERRATA.

PAGE 9—10th line, omit *or* before yet.

PAGE 10—8th line, for *insure* read *inure*.

PAGE 11—12th line, for *were* read *here*.

PAGE 14—1st line, insert *them* after *expect*.